Library of Congress Cataloging in Publication Data

Willard, Nancy.
The well-mannered balloon.

SUMMARY: James' balloon is very well-mannered until the middle of the night when it develops a voracious appetite.
[1. Balloons – Fiction] I. Shekerjian, Haig.
II. Shekerjian, Regina. III. Title.
PZ7.W6553We [E] 75-29158
ISBN 0-15-294985-2

*by the same author*

SAILING TO CYTHERA:
And Other Anatole Stories

Nancy Willard

# The Well-Mannered Balloon

illustrated by Haig & Regina Shekerjian

HARCOURT BRACE JOVANOVICH
New York and London



Printed in the United States of America

First edition

B C D E F G H I J K

1000 BALLOONS
FOR YOU
WELL-MANNERED

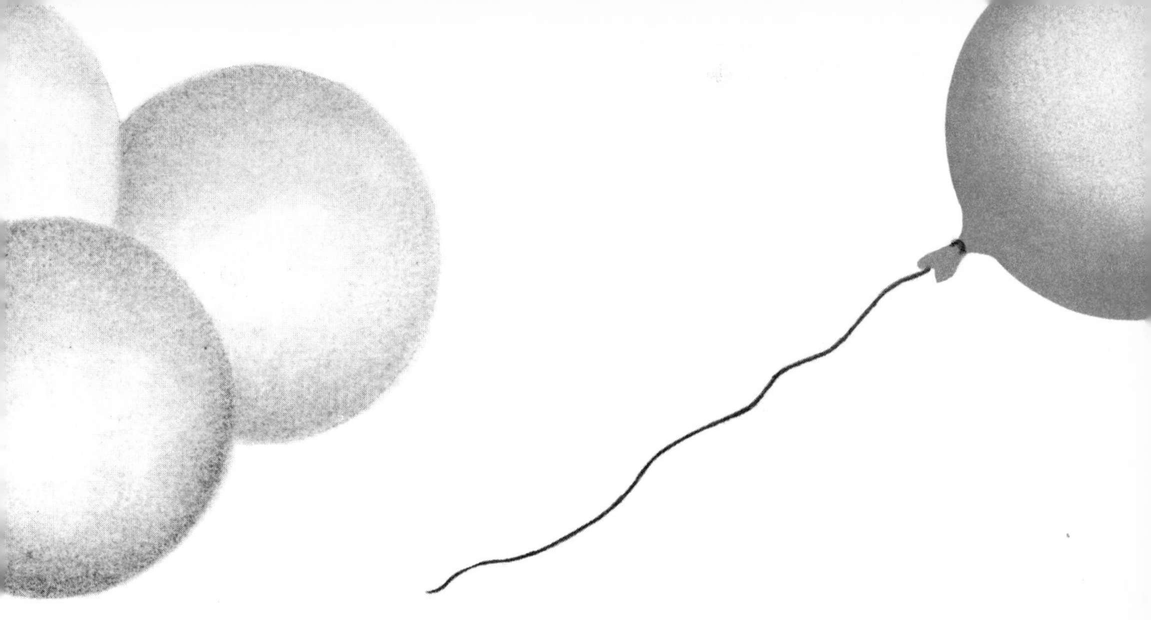

The day James and his mother went
downtown to buy him some new shoes,
whom should they meet but the balloon man.

“Please, Mother, buy me a balloon,”
said James.

“Later,” said Mother.

So after they bought some shoes, his
mother bought him a balloon,

and James carried it home.

He painted a pirate's face on it and invited the balloon to dinner.

“Can I have my ice cream right now?” asked James.

“Later,” said Mother.

The balloon ate nothing at all.

“A very well-mannered balloon,” said Father.

When James went to bed, he tied the balloon to the bedpost.

"Can I do my jumpies now?" asked James.

"Later," said Mother.

"Can I have a glass of water?" asked James.

"Later," said Mother.

JAMES
JACKS
G·G·
FUN

The balloon did not
do jumpies in bed.

It did not ask for a glass of water.

"A very well-mannered balloon,"
said Mother.

Then Mother went to bed and Father
went to bed.

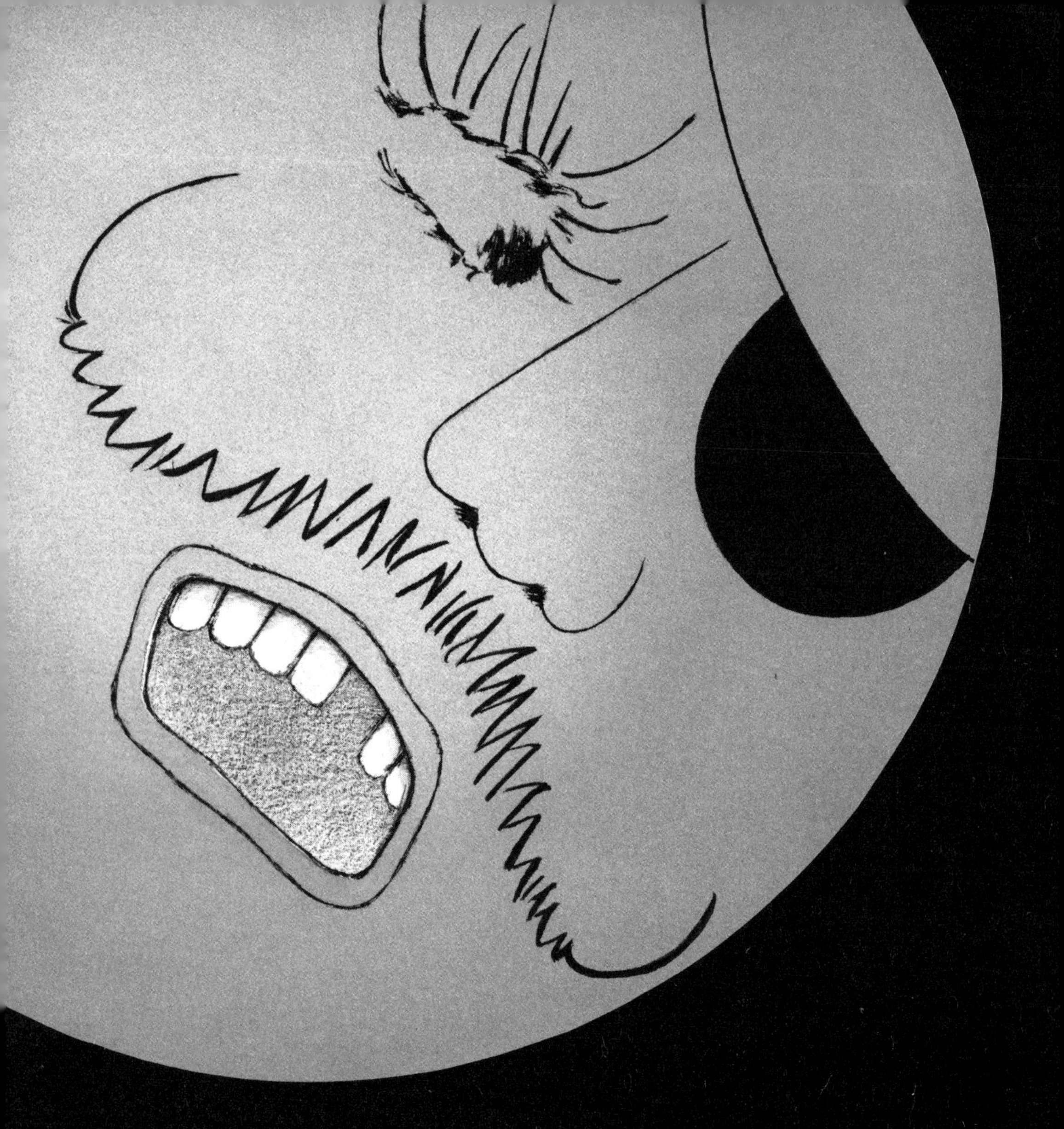

And the balloon spoke in a very ill-mannered voice.

“Wake up,” said the balloon. “I’m thirsty.”

So James climbed out of bed and brought the balloon a glass of water.

"I want milk," said the balloon.

So James took the balloon downstairs to the kitchen and poured it a glass of milk.

But the balloon drank not just *one* glass of milk but *all* the milk.

Then it gobbled up all the milk bottles
and all the drinking glasses
and all the cups and all
the napkins.

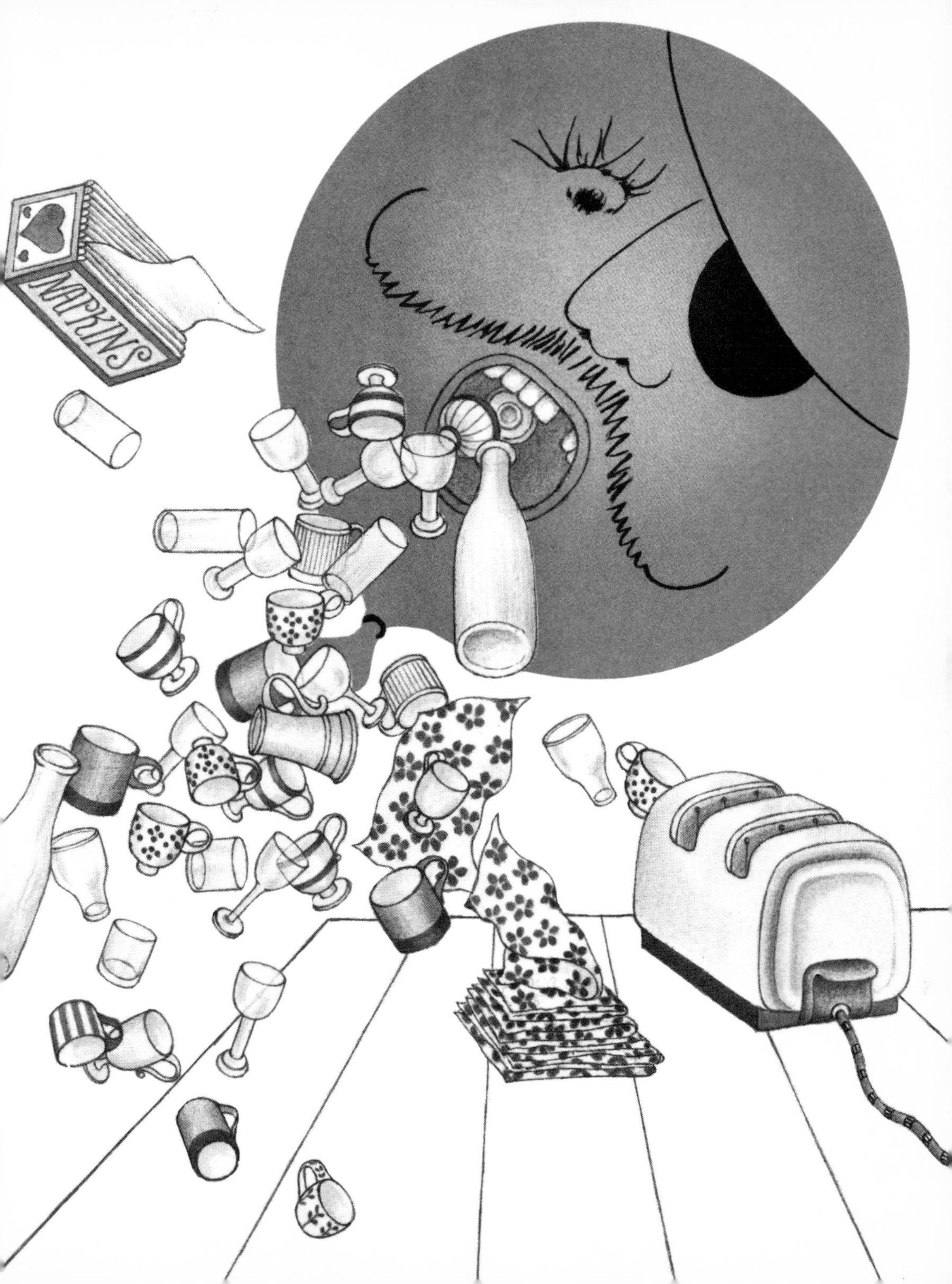
NAPKINS

“I’m hungry,”
said the balloon.

“Have a banana,” said James.

But the balloon ate not just *one* banana but *all* the bananas.

Then it ate the apples and the pears
and then it ate the plate.

And then it ate all the plates
and all four boxes of raisins
and a box of soda crackers.

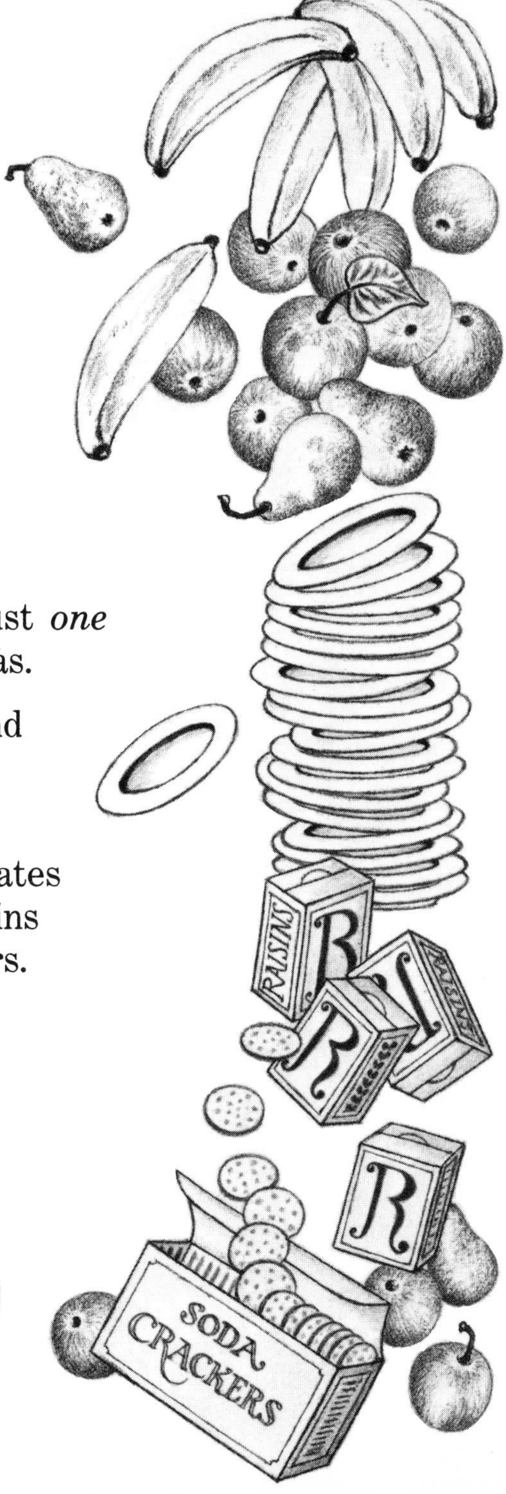

"And now I'm really hungry," said the balloon.

"I'll toast you some bread," said James.

But the balloon ate not just *one* slice of bread but *all* the bread and the butter, and then it ate the butter dish and a box of salt and a five-pound bag of sugar and two jars of honey and five jars of raspberry jam.

Then it ate the toaster.

"Yum," said the balloon.

"Oh, my," said James.

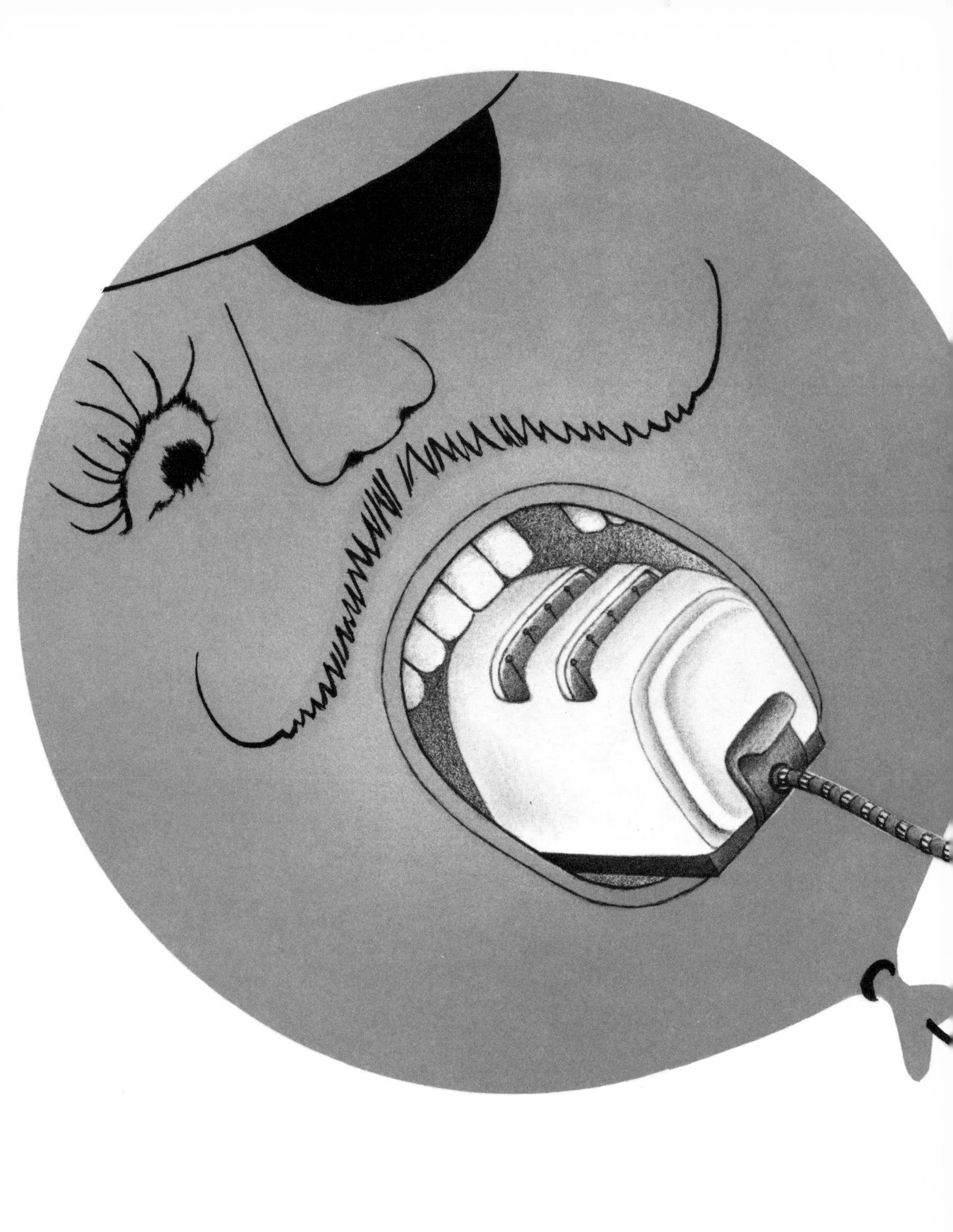

"And now I'm really VERY hungry,"
said the balloon.

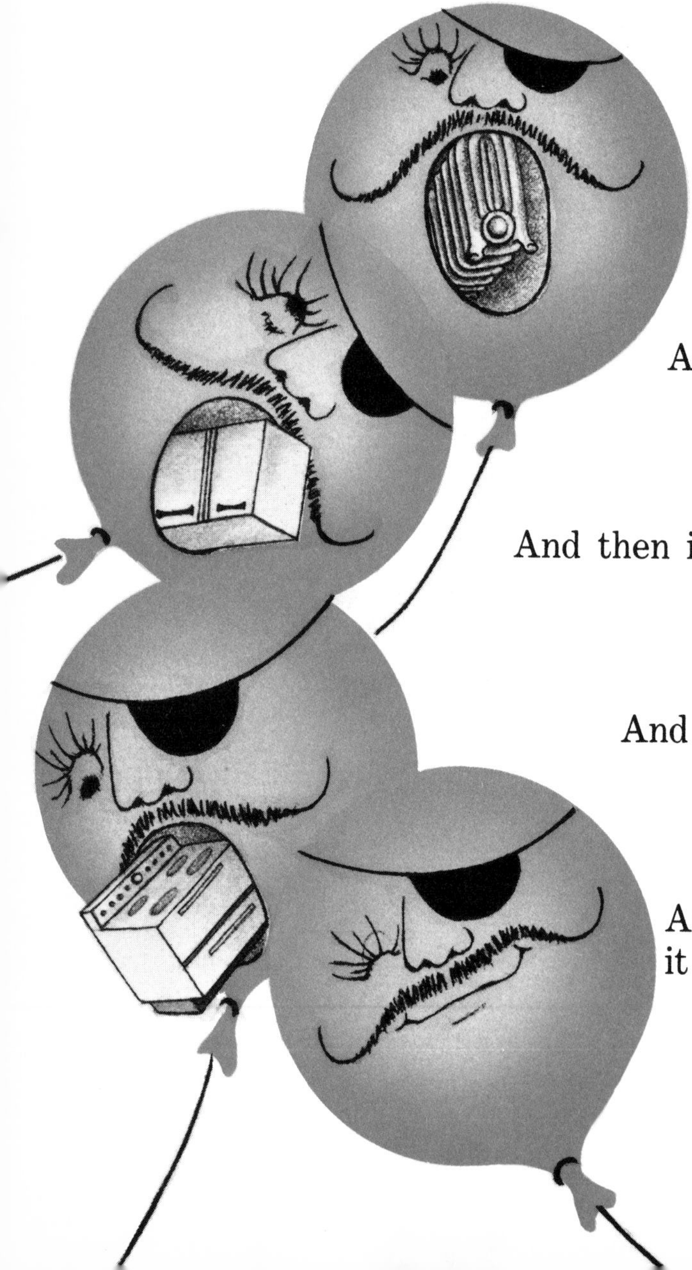

And it ate the radiator.

And then it ate the refrigerator.

And then it ate the stove.

And then, just for fun,
it ate the kitchen table.

“And now,” said the balloon,
“I’m going to eat YOU up.”

“Wait,” said James. “I’ll bet you’ve never eaten a giant strawberry with silver sprinkles.”

"No," said the balloon, "I haven't."

"Oh, there's nothing more delicious than a giant strawberry with silver sprinkles," said James.

"Yum," said the balloon. "Give me a giant strawberry with silver sprinkles."

So James fetched his mother's pincushion from her sewing basket and served it to the balloon on a silver platter.

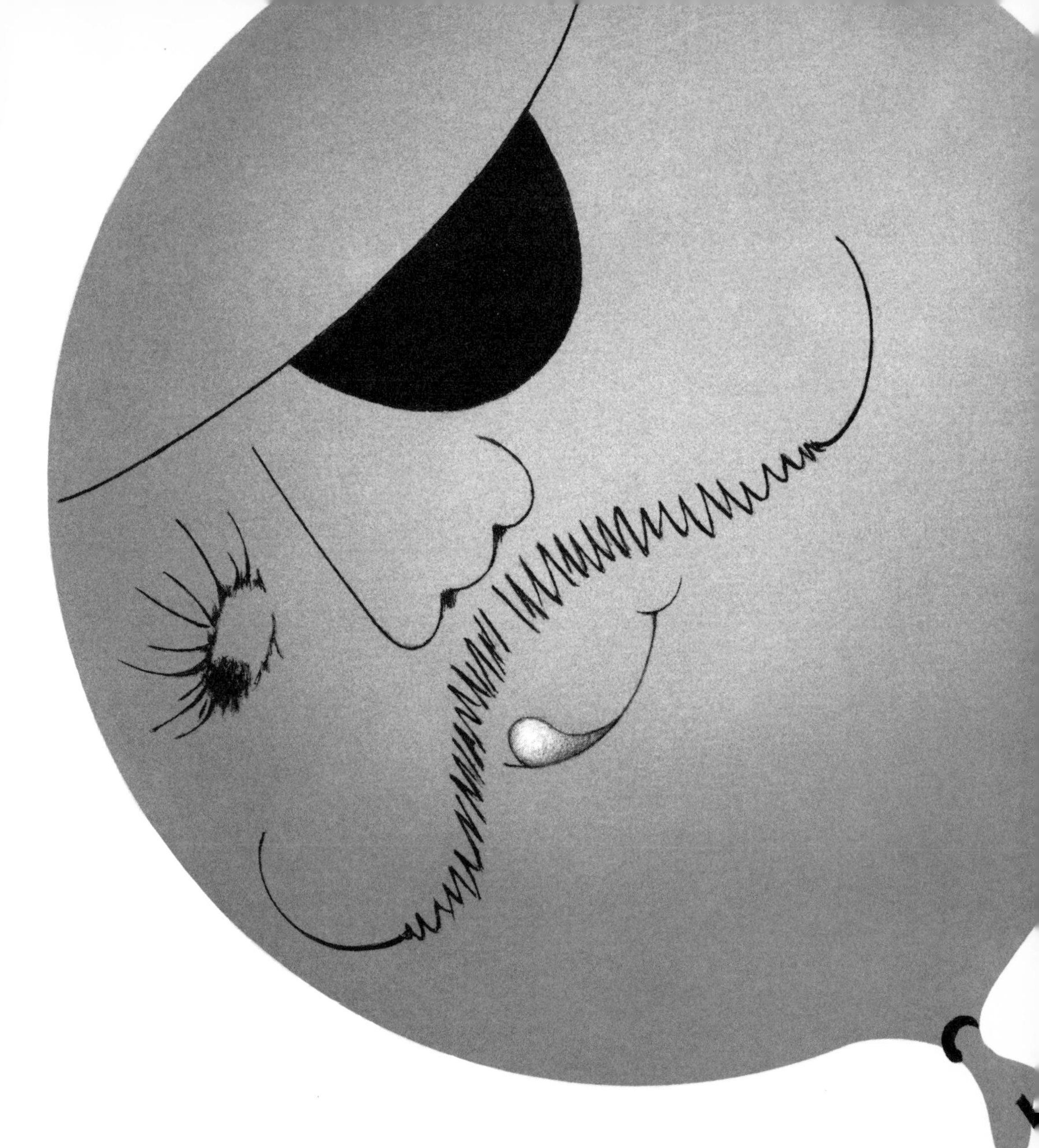

And the balloon swallowed the pincushion.

POP
SALT
IODIZED
SODA
CKERS
BUTTER

Out sprang the milk bottles, the drinking glasses, the cups,
the napkins,
the bananas,

the apples,
the pears,
the plates,
the four boxes of raisins,
the box of soda crackers,
the bread and the butter,
the butter dish,

the box of salt,
the five-pound bag of sugar,
the two jars of honey and the five jars of raspberry jam,
the toaster,
the radiator,
the refrigerator, the stove,
and the kitchen table.

And James went back to bed.

STORIES
MAGIC

The next morning his mother found the broken balloon.

"Oh, what a pity that you broke your balloon! But I'm going downtown again today. Can I bring you another one just like it?"

“Later,”
said James.